The Monkey's Tale

by Jeremy Strong

illustrated by Mike Spoor

Contents

PEARSON
Longman

Text © Jeremy Strong 2003
Series editors: Martin Coles and Christine Hall

PEARSON EDUCATION LIMITED
Edinburgh Gate
Harlow
Essex CM20 2JE
England

www.longman.co.uk

First published 2003
ISBN 0582 79610 5

Illustrated by Mike Spoor

Printed in Great Britain by Scotprint, Haddington

The publishers' policy is to use paper manufactured from sustainable forests.

1 Escape!

"The monkey's escaped!" yelled Mr Luke at his assistant, Tara. "Look, he's on the parrot cage. Quick! Shut the front door before he runs out."

Tara ran to the pet shop door and closed it with a bang. The door almost flattened Mrs Rafello's nose. She jumped back a step, giving Tara an astonished look through the glass. All she wanted was a tin of dog food.

"Sorry!" said Tara. "The monkey's escaped!"

Mrs Rafello couldn't hear her through the glass. "What did you say?" she shouted back. But of course Tara couldn't hear Mrs Rafello either.

"What did you say?" Tara shouted at Mrs Rafello.

"What did you say?" Mrs Rafello bellowed back.

Heaven knows how long this might have gone on if Mr Luke hadn't called Tara over to help him.

The monkey was still on top of the cage, looking very lively, his bright, cheeky eyes shiny with mischief. Tara watched anxiously as Mr Luke reached up to the chocolate-coloured animal.

"Mind he doesn't bite you," she warned.

Mr Luke laughed. "Ziggy wouldn't hurt a fly, would you? Come on down, you rascal."

The owner of the pet shop stretched out his arms. The monkey banged his little fists on the big cage and startled an African grey parrot, who gave a loud, angry squawk. It took a lightning peck at Ziggy's long tail. This did not help Mr Luke at all.

The monkey took off in alarm, and made a great leap from the cage. But Ziggy had paid no attention to the direction of his jump. He landed with his back legs in one of the fish tanks. Ziggy yelped and water slopped over the sides. The fish began to zoom round and round the tanks.

Mr Luke stumbled after him, struggling over grain sacks and boxes. Everything seemed to get in his way. The birds flapped and fluttered and squeaked. The hamsters all took to their wheels and paddled away as if they had just been turbo charged.

Tara, who was supposed to be helping, just stood there with both hands over her mouth and her eyes popping. On the far side of the door Mrs Rafello now had her nose pressed hard against the glass as she tried to see what was going on.

"Will you get out of my way?" demanded a small old lady. She had a tiny white poodle on a tiny white lead. "I want to go in there."

"But there's a ..." began Mrs Rafello.

The little old lady interrupted. "Don't just stand there blocking the door. My poodle needs some shampoo. Just look at his muddy paws. Please move out of the way."

Inside the shop Mr Luke was having a hard time. "Ow!" he cried as he banged his leg, leaping over a rabbit hutch. "The pesky thing. Ziggy, come here!"

The little monkey was beginning to enjoy himself. It was a long time since he had been able to stretch his legs. He clattered up on top of the birdcages and sat there, just above the canaries. He looked down at Mr Luke with his black, shining eyes and scratched an itchy cheek with one slender finger.

Mr Luke stopped and sighed. "Fetch the ladder, Tara. I'll have to climb up and get him."

Tara fetched the small steps and opened them out. Mr Luke began to climb shakily towards Ziggy, while Tara held the steps steady. The monkey watched with grave interest. What a game this was! It was at this moment that the little old lady with the poodle finally managed to push Mrs Rafello to one side. She shoved the door open and in she walked, with her tiny white poodle tripping along at her feet.

"Good afternoon," she began. "I'd like to … Eeek! Help! A giant spider!"

She screeched even louder than the parrot, and Ziggy leaped for the open door.

He flew through the air and landed right beside

the poodle. The astonished dog dashed wildly round and round the old lady, tying up her legs with the dog lead.

"Help!" she cried again as she began to sway dangerously. Mr Luke rushed over just in time to catch her.

And while Mr Luke untangled the old lady and the poodle yapped and jumped up and down and Tara just stared in amazement, Ziggy made his escape.

2 Pandemonium!

The monkey scampered out onto the street and suddenly his world was full of flashing feet and scooping hands, yells and screams and shouts. Enormous hands tried to seize him. His tail was grabbed and pulled, but each time he managed to wriggle away. He was almost kicked across the pavement as a man tried to stop him with his foot.

Ziggy darted away, chattering angrily. He leaped and danced and hopped and ran. He scampered up pushchairs and onto people's shoulders, jumping from one head to another as if they were stepping-stones. He seemed to be everywhere at once.

Cars and buses and lorries screeched and honked all around as Ziggy skipped across the road. The traffic came to a complete stop as Ziggy danced over the bonnets and roofs, twanging aerials and swinging on mirrors.

Angry drivers tried to shoo him away. Ziggy chattered back at them just as angrily, showing his sharp little teeth. The drivers wound up their windows and glared at the monkey.

On the other side of the road Ziggy found himself in the shopping centre. He dashed in and out of doorways, while Mr Luke struggled behind, trying to catch up. Ziggy scampered into a shoe shop, knocked over two big displays and came out again, waving a large hiking boot.

"Come here!" yelled Mr Luke.

Ziggy threw the boot at him and took off again. Suddenly he saw a large pile of bananas on the greengrocer's stall. Ziggy jumped up.

"Hey you! Get away from those," cried the greengrocer.

Ziggy seized a tomato and threw it at the greengrocer. He ducked and it hit a passer-by instead. There was a lot more shouting and Ziggy got so scared he felt he had to throw as many tomatoes as possible – so he did. When he ran out of tomatoes, he threw courgettes and oranges.

Even so, Mr Luke was closing in. But just as he reached out towards Ziggy the furious greengrocer rushed at the monkey waving a large broom. Ziggy was off again in a flash.

Away and away he ran, his long legs pounding at the pavement. He twisted, turned and leaped through the crowd. Everywhere there was noise and confusion. He seemed to make a thousand escapes. No matter which way he turned there were hands reaching for him.

Mr Luke and Tara were still huffing and puffing after him, followed by a long line of excited people. Each one had a good idea about how to catch the little monkey.

"Shoot him with a stun gun!"

"Use a fishing net!"

"Dig a trap for him!"

Ziggy was rapidly tiring. All this jumping and

leaping and excitement had worn him out. He was only a small creature and couldn't keep up this level of activity forever. He reached the end of the high street. Up ahead he could begin to make out grass and trees offering secret hideaways among their leafy branches. He had reached the edge of the town. He jumped away through the bushes, and the grass closed around him so that only the tip of his brown tail could be seen, moving across the field like a super-speedy beetle.

Mr Luke stopped by the woods and looked sadly into the trees. "We'll never catch him now," he panted. "Poor Ziggy."

A young girl who had joined in the chase looked up brightly at Mr Luke. "He'll be all right," she said. "He can live in the trees."

Mr Luke smiled at her. "Oh yes, he can live in the trees all right. Ziggy will enjoy that. But there's no food for him out there. He eats oranges and bananas and things like that. And what happens when he meets a fox or a weasel?"

Mr Luke shook his head sadly. "I hope somebody finds him," he murmured. "He'll find it hard on his own."

3 Peace

Ziggy swung easily through the trees, as if he had
never lived in a cage. It was late summer and the
days were warm. His dark coat was glossy and
thick, his eyes bright with curious interest in
everything around him. He picked at leaves and
poked his fingers into holes. He grabbed an old
bird's nest and stuck it on his head. All he could
hear was the slow rustle of the wind amongst the
leaves and the singing of birds.

Evening came and Ziggy grew tired. He looked
around for his warm cage, expecting it to be
there, as it always had been in the shop. He was
puzzled. Ziggy spent half an hour hunting for his
cage with its warm pile of straw for bedding. But
he didn't find it.

At last his instincts took over and he climbed
high into a beech tree and began to pull twigs and
leaves together. He built himself a platform of

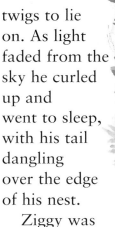

twigs to lie on. As light faded from the sky he curled up and went to sleep, with his tail dangling over the edge of his nest.

Ziggy was lucky. The nights were not at all cold yet.

In the middle of the night he was startled by a loud hoot. Ziggy leaped to his feet and stared out at the inky darkness. There was a flutter above and the owl hooted again. Ziggy almost toppled from his branch. The owl was surprised too and quickly swooped away, leaving the monkey still staring out, trying to discover what all the noise had been about. Then he fell back asleep.

Ziggy woke early the next morning. He was hungry and looking forward to the bowl of fruit that Mr Luke brought him every morning. But there was no fruit, just as there had been no warm cage. He spent most of that morning up the tree, too nervous to move very far. By midday the sun was high and Ziggy's stomach ached with hunger. He realised he would have to find food for himself.

He searched the trees for fruit, but all he found were some spiders and a few caterpillars. He chewed on them, wrinkling his face until he looked a hundred years old, then spat them out violently. He hurriedly chewed a few leaves to get rid of the taste.

Ziggy took to the ground and at last he had
some good luck. First of all he found a small
bramble patch. Most of the blackberries were
unripe but the monkey didn't mind. He moved
slowly from one bush to the next. His mouth was
soon stained with the dark juice of the berries. As
he reached the last bush a much more interesting
sight met his eyes.

Ziggy was right beside an apple orchard. In a
flash he was up among the knobbly branches and
stuffing himself. He was a tidy eater. He even
swallowed the apple cores.

That night Ziggy
returned to his nest
tired and full and happy.
He threw away his old bedding and
made up a new platform. Soon he
was asleep and not even the
hooting owl disturbed his rest.

Many more days followed like this. The wood
became more and more familiar to him, and he
was not so nervous. Every day Ziggy visited the
orchard and fed from the apples. The puzzled
farmer wondered why all
the trees near the wood had so
few apples. He never caught
sight of the little monkey,
chewing steadily.

Ziggy did not notice the slow-falling
leaves and the shortening days. The
weather was still warm and kind.
But winter was on its way, and
Ziggy did not know about
winter or the snow and hunger
and the hunting animals that it
would bring.

4 A Nasty Shock

One late October morning two children came wandering by. They had a garden next to the wood and they often went exploring. Ziggy stayed high in his tree, watching them closely with his black, curious eyes.

Daniel and Jess passed right beneath him. If he had kept quiet the children would never have noticed him, but Ziggy started beating his chest and making loud "whoop-whoop" noises. It was what he had done whenever children came into the pet shop. It made them giggle, and the monkey liked the noise children made when they laughed.

Jess stared up. She grabbed Daniel's arm. "Look – a monkey! It's a monkey!"

The children stared with open mouths while Ziggy sat on his branch, whooping. He snatched up several twigs and threw them down at the delighted children.

"A real monkey! I'm going to get him," declared Daniel.

"You can't climb that tree. The branches are too high."

"If you bend down I could step on your back."

Jess bent down and Daniel climbed up. "Ow! You weigh more than an elephant!" She straightened up and rubbed her shoulders as Daniel scrambled into the tree.

Ziggy watched carefully as Daniel picked his way among the branches. His black eyes sparkled. He had been quite bored on his own in the wood, but this was fun! He grabbed handfuls of beechnuts and chucked them at Daniel so that some bounced off his head.

Ziggy waited until Daniel had almost reached him, then all at once he swung away, whooping. He vanished with a crashing of leaves and shaking of branches.

Daniel slowly returned to the ground. "I almost got him," he said glumly.

Jess grinned. "You've got twigs stuck in your hair," she pointed out.

When the children got home they told their mother all about Ziggy, but of course she didn't believe them. She said it must have been a squirrel. When Jess and Daniel insisted it was a monkey Mum got cross and told them to stop arguing. Daniel and Jess looked at each other and sighed. They couldn't really blame Mum. After all it was unusual to have a monkey scampering about in the wood. They decided to go back the next day and see if they could find him again.

When Daniel went to bed, his head filled with cunning plans for catching monkeys.

"It's quite easy really," he told Jess the next morning, and she nodded. Daniel always thought things would be quite easy. Jess had noticed that things that seemed easy to him often turned out to be really difficult.

As it happened, it was a little while before Daniel and Jess could return to the wood, and in the meantime a lot of things happened to Ziggy. First of all, he visited the apple orchard, but he found that there were no apples. The farmer had picked them and sent them all to the shops. Ziggy rushed round the orchard but found nothing.

He went and searched for blackberries, but they

had long since finished. When evening came his stomach was still empty.

Winter was on its way. That night the weather changed. Quite suddenly it became cold. Ziggy shivered in his nest. Then it began to rain. He had been rained on before, but this was cold, hard rain. It pushed through the leaves with cold, wet fingers and poked down into Ziggy's tangled fur.

Ziggy crouched down. He couldn't find shelter. The weak leaves were plucked off by the steady rain. They tumbled down and stuck to Ziggy's matted fur.

23

He was miserable. It was very dark, but Ziggy could not stay out all night in such cold rain. He left his nest and slipped down to the ground and started to hunt for dry shelter. He splashed through the mud and the puddles. A startled rabbit ran across his path.

Suddenly the air around the monkey was full of menace. There was nothing to be seen, nothing to be heard or smelled, but Ziggy could sense an enormous, terrifying danger.

He froze, his big ears trying to catch the sound of something; something close by. He did not know what it was. If it hadn't been raining Ziggy would have heard the fox. If it hadn't been raining Ziggy would have smelled the fox. But the rain drowned everything.

There was a sudden snarl and crunching snap of strong jaws.

Ziggy jumped with sheer terror, springing round to meet the big dog-fox. A pair of green, slit eyes burned out at the small monkey. The fox tensed his muscles and leaped again.

Ziggy yelped as the fox grazed one ear. He lashed out with his own little paws and the fox gave a shrill whine as Ziggy caught him on the nose.

For a moment the fox hesitated. Ziggy took his opportunity, turned tail and fled, darting up the nearest tree. Right to the top he went, while the fox set his paws against the trunk and snarled.

The fox sniffed several times at the tree and then skulked away into the night.

5 Meeting the Neighbours

Ziggy clung to a branch, shivering with cold and fear, while the rain continued to fall like tiny, sharp arrows. He stayed up there the rest of the night, too frightened to move. Hours later, as the sun began to put a bit of pale light back into the sky, Ziggy stretched his soaked and aching body and shook the water from his fur. It had stopped raining, but the air was chill.

The monkey set out to find food. He was wet and he was cold. Every time he swung on a branch another shower of raindrops pelted him. All morning heavy grey clouds shut out the warmth of the sun and Ziggy hardly managed to dry out at all. He came down to the ground and wandered through the mud, daintily picking up his feet and shaking off the water with each step.

Ziggy, still searching for food, popped his head round the base of a tree and almost clunked heads

with a grey squirrel. The two animals
chattered with alarm, leaping back from
each other before stopping to take a more
curious look. Ziggy had never seen a
squirrel before, and the squirrel had
certainly never seen a
monkey.

They gazed at each other warily. Ziggy sat
back, watching and waiting. He scratched his
bottom, pretending that he wasn't actually
looking at the squirrel. The squirrel ran to a tree,
but when the monkey just sat still she didn't
bother to go up.

Bit by bit, small jump by small jump, the
squirrel came back to the patch of ground she had
been heading for. She had nuts buried there and

she wanted to dig them up. The strange creature
was examining his feet, and didn't seem interested
in her, so the squirrel decided it was safe after all.
She scrabbled quickly in the ground, unearthing
her little store.

Ziggy was fascinated. This was most
interesting. You dug in the ground and there were
nuts, hiding there, ready to be eaten. Amazing!
Ziggy was a fast learner. He had just learned a
new way to find food and he was pleased with
himself. The ground was full of nuts! If only he
had known earlier.

Ziggy watched for ten minutes as the squirrel
munched her way through the little store, then off
she went, back up a tree. Ziggy took his chance

and hurried across to the disturbed ground. He
scrabbled around with his paws, expecting to find
a harvest of nuts, but he could not find a
single one. He tried another patch, and
then another. He scratched at the earth
faster and faster, becoming more and
more frustrated and cross.

Ziggy seized a big stick. He jumped in
the air and began hitting the
ground angrily. Jump! Bang!
Jump! Bang!
Jump! Bang!
All at once
the stick
broke in
half,
leaving him
holding a stump
while the other
bit went
cartwheeling
up into the air
before coming
back down
and hitting
him on the
head.

Ow! The monkey leaped away and scampered through the trees, hungry and miserable. All morning he wandered through the wood looking for food. His tail drooped behind him. His fur was splattered with mud. His head hurt.

He found a pile of round black berries, or maybe they were nuts. He looked around, half expecting a squirrel to leap out and lay claim to them. He was not at all sure that you could

eat these things, but there was only one way he could find out. He gingerly picked one up and popped it into his mouth.

One bite was quite enough. Urgh! Ziggy pulled a disgusted face and spat it out as far as he could. Rabbit pellets were definitely not good!

When he reached the
edge of the wood he
discovered a large
garden. He trotted across
the lawn. There was
something on the bird table. It
looked like bread.

Ziggy jumped onto the table and a
crowd of sparrows took to the air, chirping
angrily. Ziggy crouched on the table and tried
chewing a crust. Then he hauled up a string of
nuts and cracked some open with his teeth. It
wasn't much, but it was a lot better than he'd had
for a long time.

Jess was in the kitchen of the
house and she looked up
when she heard the sparrows.
"The monkey's in the garden!"
she yelled. "Look, Mum, it really is
a monkey!"

6 Is That a Trap?

Mum and Daniel hurried to the window. "Well, just take a look at that!" Mum cried. "What on earth is a monkey doing in our back garden? It must be frozen."

Jess tugged at Mum's sleeve. "If we put out some food we may be able to catch it," she suggested.

"Good idea," Mum agreed. So they cut up some fruit and carried the bits out to the bird table. As soon as he saw them Ziggy dashed away, chattering and whooping madly. He beat his chest and did a rather good back flip, making the two children laugh.

"Let's go back inside and watch from the kitchen," said Mum. "I'm sure he'll come back."

As soon as everyone had returned to the house Ziggy did come back. He was very hungry and he couldn't stay away for long. He swung himself up onto the bird table and sat there and ate all the food.

The children watched with delight. They kept sneaking outside and adding more treats to the bird table – some bits of orange, half an apple and a whole banana. Ziggy would dance away in alarm but come racing back as soon as the children went back inside. He filled his stomach, while Daniel and Jess watched from the window and hatched their plans for catching the monkey.

"If we catch him can we keep him?" asked Daniel.

"Well, I don't know. He must belong to someone," Mum pointed out.

"Yeah, well, they don't deserve him. They let him escape and if he stays in the woods all winter he'll die, because he doesn't know how to survive in snow. I mean he can't ski or anything."

"Daniel! Monkeys don't ski!" laughed Jess.

"Exactly," Daniel went on. "If he *could* ski he'd be all right, but he can't so what's he going to do? He'll die! We've got to look after him."

"I'm not so sure," said Mum. "Like I said, he must belong to someone and I have a feeling that they will probably turn up sooner or later, so don't raise your hopes. Anyhow, the poor thing has to be caught first of all."

"Oh, that'll be easy," declared Daniel.

Jess gave a quiet sigh. Now where had she heard *that* before?

Every day after that Ziggy returned to the garden. It was much better than digging up the ground trying to find a few nuts. All he had to do was turn up at the garden and there was the bird table, piled high with food. It was just like being back at the pet shop, except that he was free!

But there was another side to being free. The nights were getting awfully cold. But never mind, there was the bird table, full of food again!

Over the next few days Daniel and his father invented all kinds of traps to try and capture the wild monkey. But Ziggy was far too clever. No matter what they did Ziggy seemed to be one jump ahead of them.

Dad put a bowl of fruit under a big box that was propped up by a stick tied to a long piece of string.

Ziggy stared at the fruit and the box and the string for a long time. If he went under the box to get the fruit then Dad would pull out the stick. So Ziggy got a stick for himself. He knocked down the box, then lifted up one corner and grabbed the fruit. Dad had to laugh.

Daniel reckoned he had a better idea. He dug a small pit and covered it over. The pit was right beside the bird table, where Ziggy always walked. Ziggy sniffed at the pit.

He poked a slender finger through the covering and waggled it about. Hmmm, very odd. There was definitely something strange going on here. He found a big stone and rolled it onto twigs covering the pit so that they gave way. The stone crashed into the trap below.

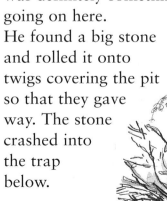

The monkey chattered and whooped and ran back into the wood, taking an armful of banana and apple bits with him. He had escaped again.

But Ziggy was not clever enough to escape the weather. Each day seemed a little colder than the one before. The leaves had long gone from the trees, so he had nothing to snuggle down in. He had managed to find a hole, high in a tree, but it offered no protection from the piercing wind and the frost. He crept in there and shivered right the way through the night.

Then the snow came – a hard first fall. The icy flakes flickered past the monkey's dull eyes. He sneezed, shivered and wiped a small paw across his wrinkled face. Ziggy was ill.

7 Trouble

Ziggy was used to being warm and looked after. Now he huddled down low in his hollow tree and shivered and sneezed. Every morning he was weaker than the day before, and it was a struggle to get to the garden to eat.

"He's so thin," whispered Daniel one morning, as Ziggy sat in the snow and chewed slowly on a courgette. "Isn't there anything we can do?"

"We can't help him unless we can catch him, and he won't let us do that," murmured Mum.

That same afternoon the snow fell again. Ziggy watched it from his tree. It slowly lined the edge of his hole until there was a thick cold layer like half a front door. It snowed all through the evening and on into the night.

Ziggy couldn't sleep. His bones ached and throbbed with fever. His eyes were dull and half-closed. He lay and listened to the mournful

hooting of the night owl. He heard the high barking of the fox as it stood sniffing at the bottom of the tree. The fox could sniff out the dead and the dying. It knew when there was a creature in trouble, and a creature in trouble usually made a very good meal for a hungry fox. Ziggy's blood ran colder still.

When morning came the snow had changed everything. It was a different wood. Ziggy dragged himself out onto a branch and stared with watery eyes at the strange scene. He sat up there a long time, trying to find the strength to climb down and reach the garden.

He was only half-way down the tree when he fell. His weak fingers no longer had the strength to grip the icy branches and he tumbled the rest of the way, crashing through the thin branches so that they whipped his little body as he plunged past them. When he hit the ground the breath was knocked from his body and he lay there, more dead than alive.

Ziggy was so ill and so very tired he might have given up there and then, and let sleep turn to unconsciousness and unconsciousness slip into death. But there was something that would not let him give up. He remembered the laughter of the children. He remembered warm sunshine and leaves and leaping amongst the trees. And he wanted more of it. Ziggy struggled upright. He must reach the garden and find food.

When at last he staggered out onto the smooth white lawn of the big garden, Daniel ran to Mum in alarm. "Quick, Mum! Look at him! He's dying!"

Mum and Daniel stared out as Ziggy tried to get to the pile of fruit they had left out for him. The little monkey lurched through the snow, stumbling, falling, picking himself up and trying to carry on. Even from the kitchen they could see he was shivering from head to toe.

"The poor thing," sighed Mum.

"We must do something," Jess said in a strange, hoarse voice. Her eyes were full of tears. She simply could not bear to watch the heroic struggle of the small creature.

"We'll only frighten him off if we go after him," Mum warned.

But it was too late. There was a gentle click from the double door that led from the back room out to the garden. Mum whirled round and was just in time to see Jess step outside. She almost shouted at her daughter to stop, but that would most certainly frighten away the monkey. All that she and Daniel could do now was hold their breath.

Jess moved slowly and quietly, one step at a time. She held her coat in front of her, not bothering to put it on, even though the flakes were steadily drifting down all around her. She reached the end of the patio and stopped at the edge of the lawn, keeping her eyes on the monkey. She was thinking, "If I keep saying in my head that he mustn't move, he mustn't move, it will work and he will stay there."

Ziggy stopped too, and looked back at the small figure standing there quietly on the other side of the snowy lawn. He didn't move. Jess held out her coat.

"Come on, monkey," she whispered, taking another step forward. "I won't hurt you." She still had her slippers on, but she didn't feel the cold snow seeping through the thin covering. Her eyes were fixed on Ziggy.

The monkey crouched low, trembling with fever. He was pitifully thin. Jess bit her lips and silently moved closer and closer. She was desperate to catch Ziggy and to carry him into the warmth of the house. Ziggy bared his teeth and gave a half-hearted snarl.

"Ssssh. I won't hurt you, little monkey. It's all right. I won't hurt you."

Just a few more steps now, a few more steps.

8 The Rightful Owner

By the kitchen door Mum and Daniel were still holding their breath. Daniel had crossed his fingers and his legs. Now Jess was standing right beside Ziggy. Ever so gently she knelt down in the snow and placed her coat around the trembling animal. She lifted the pitiful bundle into her arms and walked back into the house.

Mum was already on the telephone to the vet. He came out immediately and was quite astonished that Ziggy had survived for so long.

"It's a miracle he's still alive," said the vet seriously. "He's a very lucky animal."

"Will he be all right?" asked Daniel anxiously.

The vet nodded. "Warmth and food are what he needs most. I've given him an injection that will help him shake off that fever. He'll be all right in a few weeks, but he does need a bit of loving care. Looking at you two children I think there'll probably be plenty of that!"

So it was that Ziggy moved out of
the woods and into the house. Day
by day his strength returned,
and so did his sense of
mischief. It was great fun to
have a real monkey in
the house, but there
were times when
Mum in particular
rather wished that
Ziggy hadn't come to stay.

There was the day he sat on Dad's chocolate
birthday cake, for example.

Then there was the time he climbed up the
shower curtain while Jess was having a shower,
and managed to pull down not only the
curtain, but also the curtain rail and
a large lump of ceiling plaster.

Then there was the time Ziggy hid in the car, and they didn't discover him until they got to the supermarket. There they were, doing their shopping, when Ziggy suddenly poked his head out of Mum's shopping bag and grabbed some toilet rolls.

That might have been all right except that the toilet rolls Ziggy grabbed were at the bottom of a mountain of toilet rolls. The whole lot came crashing down. Even that might have been all right, except that Ziggy, delighted at this new game, began grabbing toilet rolls and hurling them at anyone who tried to help.

It took an awful lot of sorting out and explaining to the supermarket manager, who was not as amused as Jess and Daniel.

So Mum and Dad were often annoyed by Ziggy's antics, but Daniel and Jess loved every minute of it. It was also quite obvious that the little monkey loved them, too.

If he wasn't curled up asleep on Daniel's bed at night, then he was curled up asleep on Jess's.

He followed them wherever they went. Sometimes he took rides on their backs.

Sometimes he walked beside them, holding hands. Every so often he liked to sit on their heads, like a furry crown.

And after four weeks they took Ziggy back to the vet to see how he was recovering.

"I'm amazed," he said. "You have all done a wonderful job. Just look at him! His coat is shiny. His eyes are bright. This is a fully fit monkey you have here. I have some news for you, too. I've found out where he comes from. His name is Ziggy."

And the vet told them about Mr Luke and the pet shop. "I'll let Mr Luke know," he said.

Jess's face fell. "Oh," she murmured. "Then he isn't ours after all."

"I'm afraid not. I expect Mr Luke will be in touch," the vet said as he left.

Mum ruffled Jess's hair. "You didn't think we were going to keep a monkey in the house, surely! We have one already!" She looked straight at Daniel. He scowled back at her and turned bright pink.

"Yeah, like that's really funny, Mum," he muttered darkly.

A few days later Mr Luke called. It was the day that the children dreaded, for now Ziggy would leave them. Mr Luke watched Ziggy. The monkey was sitting in the big box Dad had made for him and examining one of Dad's wellington boots. He kept climbing inside so that only his tail could be seen, waving out of the top.

"I'm amazed," Mr Luke kept saying.

"He survived out there for so long. It's certainly
my Ziggy. He looks very much at home, doesn't
he? Well, I'm so glad he's all right." Mr Luke
turned to the door and picked up his hat. "Thank
you for letting me see him. I must be off now."

"Wait!" cried Mum. "Aren't you going to take
him?"

Mr Luke shook his head. "Oh no – I think you're better at looking after him than I am. He'll probably only escape from me again. Besides, it's not much of a life sitting in a cage all day, is it? He's got trees here and a family. He'll always come back to you. He might stay away for a night or two in the summer, but he'll always come back to where it's snug and warm. I'm glad he's found such a good home. Goodbye, Ziggy, you crazy monkey!" And Mr Luke left.

"Well!" said Mum.

"Well!" said Dad, and Ziggy emptied the flower vase over his head.